LITTLE SIMON

An imprint of Simon & Schuster Children's Publishing Division • 1230 Avenue of the Americas, New York, New York 10020 • First Little Simon paperback edition January 2015 • Copyright © 2015 by Simon & Schuster, Inc. All rights reserved, including the right of reproduction in whole or in part in any form. LITTLE SIMON is a registered trademark of Simon & Schuster, Inc., and associated colophon is a trademark of Simon & Schuster, Inc. For information about special discounts for bulk purchases, please contact Simon & Schuster Special Sales at 1-866-506-1949 or business@simonandschuster.com. The Simon & Schuster Speakers Bureau can bring authors to your live event. For more information or to book an event contact the Simon & Schuster Speakers Bureau at 1-866-248-3049 or visit our website at www.simonspeakers.com. Designed by Laura Roode. The text of this book was set in Usherwood. Manufactured in the United States of America 0418 MTN
10 9
Library of Congress Cataloging-in-Publication Data
Green, Poppy. A new friend / by Poppy Green ; Illustrated by Jennifer Bell. — First edition. pages cm. — (The adventures of Sophie Mouse ; #1) Summary: Eight-year-old Sophie Mouse is excited to return to school after the long winter break, but there is a new student—a snake—and Sophie and the other animals are afraid to sit near him, much less ask him to play with them, because they have heard snakes are awful. [1. Prejudices—Fiction. 2. Friendship—Fiction. 3. Schools—Fiction. 4. Mice—Fiction. 5. Snakes—Fiction. 6. Animals—Fiction.] I. Bell, Jennifer (Jennifer A.), 1977- illustrator. II. Title. PZ7.G82616New 2015 [Fic]—dc23   2014013608
ISBN 978-1-4814-2833-0 (hc)
ISBN 978-1-4814-2832-3 (pbk)
ISBN 978-1-4814-2834-7 (eBook)

the adventures of

SOPHIE MOUSE

1

A New Friend

By Poppy Green • Illustrated by Jennifer A. Bell

LITTLE SIMON

New York London Toronto Sydney New Delhi

Contents

chapter 1

Spring Has Sprung!

Buzz, buzz, buzzzzzzz. Outside the Mouse family's cottage, a bumblebee zipped from flower to flower.

Sitting at her easel in the sunshine, Sophie Mouse put down her paintbrush. Her eyes followed the bee. *Oh, to be able to fly,* she thought. *I could see every inch of Silverlake Forest—maybe even to the other*

*side of Forget-Me-Not Lake! I won-
der how fast a bee flies when he
really gets going. What would it be
like to fly to the schoolhouse for
the first day of school tomorrow?
What would—*

"Sophie? Sophie!" Her father's voice called out, snapping her out of her daydream. He was in the doorway of their cottage, which was nestled in between the roots of an oak tree. "Are you done with your chores?" George Mouse asked. "When you are, you can go see Mom at the bakery. She's

making nutmeg popovers today!"

Sophie's little nose twitched. She was sure she could already smell the sweet scent. Nutmeg popovers were one of her mother's specialties. At her bakery in Pine Needle Grove, Lily Mouse surely would have started making the batter at dawn, before Sophie was even awake.

Sophie hated to stop painting. It was the first spring day warm enough to paint outside! But she had a little sweeping to do if she wanted to go to the bakery.

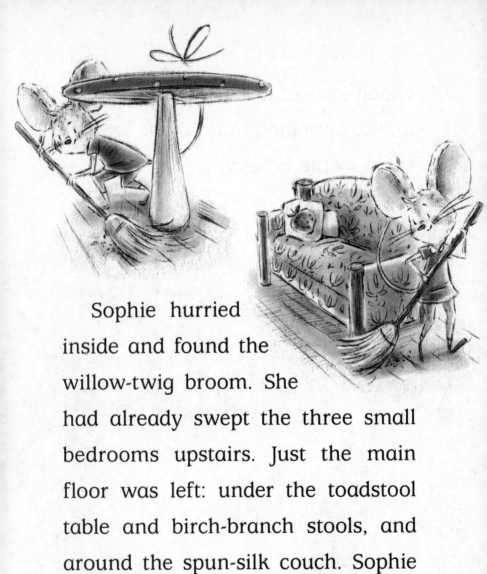

Sophie hurried inside and found the willow-twig broom. She had already swept the three small bedrooms upstairs. Just the main floor was left: under the toadstool table and birch-branch stools, and around the spun-silk couch. Sophie swept all the corners of the kitchen.

Then she swept the pile of leaf bits and dust right out the front door.

"Dad! I'm finished!" she called. "I'm going by Hattie's house on the way to the bakery!" Hattie Frog was Sophie's best friend.

Just then, way back in the rear of the cottage, a mouse's head popped up through a hole in the floor. It was Sophie's little brother, Winston. He was cleaning up the root cellar. "I want to come too!" Winston called.

Sophie sighed. Winston was six. She had been stuck inside the cottage with him for most of the winter

vacation. Now that the weather was warming up, he wanted to tag along with Sophie *everywhere*. "Have *you* finished your chores?" Mr. Mouse asked Sophie's brother.

There was a long silence. When Winston answered, his voice was quiet. "Not yet."

"Well, finish up, then," Mr. Mouse replied. "You and I can go later."

Sophie leaned her broom against the wall by the front door. Then she was off with an extra spring in her step.

It wasn't that Sophie didn't like her brother. They had fun playing together. But Sophie *was* two years older. And it was the very last day of vacation. She wanted to fill it with eight-year-old adventures! Halfway to the stream, Sophie heard a rustle in the tall reeds to her right. She stopped in her tracks.

"Hello? Is someone there?" Sophie called out.

She perked up her ears, listening carefully. But all was silent and still.

Sophie's eyes scanned the reeds.

She thought she could just make out a shadowy shape among them. She squinted and took a step closer.

Now Sophie was sure: Someone was in there.

But who was it?

chapter 2

A Perfect Day

"Harriet Frog!" Sophie called, using Hattie's full name. "Is that you in there?"

There was no answer from the reeds. So Sophie called again. "It's me—*Sophie!*"

There was a rustle. The reeds parted slowly. A green eye peeked out. Then Hattie hopped out into the open. "Phew, it *is* you," Hattie said. "I heard footsteps coming and—well, I'm glad it's you!"

Hattie was shy around strangers. But not with Sophie. They had known each other for as long as they could remember.

Sophie told Hattie about the popovers. "Want to come to the bakery?" Sophie asked. "We could stop at the lake on the way!"

Hattie giggled and shook her head. "Uh, Sophie. Forget-Me-Not Lake isn't exactly *on the way*."

Hattie is always so practical,

thought Sophie. But she was right. The lake was a bit of a hike. "Well," said Sophie, "we have lots of time. And it's our last day of vacation!"

Hattie smiled. "I'll tell my mom!" she cried, then hopped off toward home. Sophie followed and waited outside Hattie's house. It was built on the bank of the stream, not far from

Sophie's. Half the house sat floating on lily pads, right on the water. The other half was built into the pebbly bank. Sophie knew that her dad, the town architect, had helped Mr. and Mrs. Frog design it.

Soon Hattie was back and she and
Sophie were running off toward the
lake. "Please be home before dark!"
Mrs. Frog called after them.

The girls never got into too much
trouble in Silverlake Forest. Now

and then, Sophie came home with prickers on her tail or muddy clothing. One time she got lost exploring a mole tunnel. But she just asked one of the  moles for directions, and soon found her way home.

The path to Forget-Me-Not Lake was long, winding, and lined with berry bushes.

"Oh, these make the best purple paint!" Sophie exclaimed, pointing to some ripe berries. She stopped to gather some. Sophie carried pouches in her pockets at all times—for exactly this reason. Both the pouches and Sophie's pockets were always stained with berry juice.

Finally, the girls arrived at Forget-Me-Not Lake. The water glittered in the morning sun.

Sophie looked at Hattie. "Are you thinking what I'm thinking?" she asked.

"Well," Hattie said with a smile, "you do have one wild imagination,

Sophie Mouse. But if you're thinking we should go lily-pad hopping . . . hop on!"

Sophie climbed onto Hattie's back and held on tight. Hattie leaped out onto the lake. She jumped from lily pad to lily pad, hopscotching across the water. This was their very favorite thing to do at the lake.

Later, the girls made flower crowns.

They looked for four-leaf clovers. As usual, they didn't find any.

They skipped stones on the water, counting the jumps.

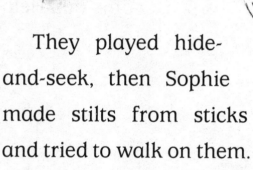

They played hide-
and-seek, then Sophie
made stilts from sticks
and tried to walk on them.

When their tummies
grumbled, it was time for popovers.

The bell on the bakery door jingled
as they entered. Mrs. Mouse was at
the counter. Several animals were

waiting patiently in line.

Sophie and Hattie scurried behind the counter just as they always did. Lily Mouse took a moment to hug them. Then she whispered, "A fresh batch of popovers just came out. Help yourselves."

The girls smiled gleefully and hurried back into the kitchen.

As they nibbled their popovers, Sophie sighed happily. It was turning out to be a great last day of vacation. Already she was thinking about the picture she would paint about it. She'd be sure to use her new purple berry paint!

chapter 3

School Surprise

The next morning, dressed in her best jumper dress and leggings, Sophie hurried to get her backpack ready. She was eager to see friends she hadn't seen all winter. *Plus,* she thought, *you never know exactly what will happen on a first day of school!*

Sophie zipped up her backpack.

"Bye, Dad!"
Sophie called as
she hurried out the door.

"Wait for me!" Winston
cried. He ran out after her, his shoe-
laces still untied.

Sophie had almost forgotten:
Winston was starting school this
year! Mrs. Wise's one-room school,
Silverlake Elementary, was for all
students ages six to ten.

Sophie bent down to tie Winston's shoes. "Mrs. Wise will want you to learn to tie these yourself," she said firmly. Then, in a gentler voice, she added, "Come on. I'll show you the *fun* way to school."

Instead of taking the path into Pine Needle Grove—past the bakery, the library, and the post office—Sophie led Winston to a little-known trail. It cut behind the library and ran through a tunnel of honeysuckle branches. The flower buds were just

opening. Sophie could hear Winston
behind her, taking deep breaths of
the scent.

The trail came out in the school-
yard. Sophie led Winston up to the
front door and inside the pine-bough
schoolhouse.

"Sophie!" Hattie's voice rang out. Sophie turned and waved. Hattie was standing with her big sister, Lydie, and their friend Ellie the squirrel. Just then, Piper the hummingbird and Zoe the bluebird flew in through the

windows. Willy the toad was already sitting at a desk next to Malcolm the mole.

And Ben the rabbit and his little brother, James, entered the room behind Sophie and Winston. Winston

knew James from preschool. So they
went off to find two desks together—
a mouse-size one for Winston and a
bigger one for James.

Sophie headed over to say hello to
Hattie, Lydie, and Ellie. But just then,
Mrs. Wise, a neatly dressed owl with
glasses, stood up at the front of the

room. "Class!" she said. "Please take your seats!"

Sophie hurried to get a maple-bark desk by a window so she could see outside. She loved looking out the window— even if Mrs. Wise *did* catch her daydreaming sometimes.

"Welcome back to school!" said Mrs. Wise when the students were seated. "I'm happy to see you all bright-eyed and ready to start

another season. Now, I think we're all here—" Mrs. Wise counted the students. "Oh! We're missing our *new* student. His family has just moved to Pine Needle Grove. His name is Owen. I know you will all make him feel very welcome."

At that moment, the door creaked open.

"Here he is now!" said Mrs. Wise. "Welcome, Owen."

All the students turned in their

seats—and gasped. Ellie and Malcolm
both let out little squeaks. Ben's ears
stood straight up. Sophie rubbed her
eyes to make sure she was seeing
this right.

Owen was . . . a *snake*?!

chapter 4

First-Day Jitters

Sophie glanced at Hattie, who was sitting behind her. Their eyes met. Sophie could tell that Hattie was just as nervous and surprised as she was.

A real snake . . . in real life! Sophie thought. She'd never seen one before. She bet none of her classmates had, either.

"Come in, Owen," Mrs. Wise said

to him warmly. "Find a seat."

Everyone watched as Owen respectfully took off his brimmed cap. Then he slithered up the center

aisle. He passed up an empty desk next to Sophie's. She breathed a sigh of relief. She didn't want to be rude, but she didn't know if she wanted Owen to sit next to her, either.

Some of Sophie's ideas about snakes came from books. But most had come from stories—spooky stories that older animals told about

poisonous sea snakes or hissing ghost snakes. Surely they couldn't be true . . . could they?

Owen found a desk
in an empty row.
Mrs. Wise began
the math lesson.
Other students took
out their notebooks.

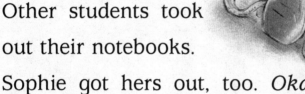

Sophie got hers out, too. *Okay. A snake in class,* she thought. *No big deal, I guess.*

Then, during quiet reading time, Sophie heard a *"Pssst."* She looked up. Owen was leaning toward Zoe's desk, which was in front of his. He was trying to get her attention. But Zoe was lost in her book.

Owen said "*Psssssst,*" a little
louder. Zoe didn't hear.

Owen tried one more time.
"*Psssssssst,*" he said loudly. Startled,
Zoe fluttered up and out of her seat,
turning to glare at Owen.

"Why are you hissing at me?" she demanded.

Owen cleared his throat. "Your bookmark is on the floor," he said. His voice was a little raspy, but gentle.

Zoe picked up her bookmark and sat down. "Oh," she said quietly. "Thanks."

At recess, Owen passed by the swing set and accidentally swatted the swing James was on with the end of his tail. The swing went flying way too high.

"Whoooooaaaa!" James cried out. "Help me!" he shouted.

James's brother, Ben, hurried over to help him down. As he did, Ben snapped at Owen, "You need to be more careful!"

Owen looked very embarrassed. "Sorry," he said quietly. "It was an accident." He slithered over to a bench and coiled up, all alone.

Sophie saw it all from across the yard. She was playing hopscotch with Hattie, Lydie, and Willy. "Hey!" Sophie said to them. "Should we ask Owen to play?"

Willy shrugged, but said nothing. Lydie didn't seem so sure. "Can snakes even hop?" she asked.

Hattie patted Sophie on the back. "I think it's a good idea," she said. "But I'm afraid to ask him. *You* ask him."

Sophie took a deep breath. She started walking over to the bench.

Then Owen looked up and saw her coming. Sophie lost her nerve and turned around.

Silly Sophie! she scolded herself. *Why are you so nervous?*

She tried to work up the courage to try again. But before she could, recess was over and it was time to go inside.

After school, Sophie and Winston got ready to walk home together. "So what did you think of school?" Sophie asked her brother as they walked out the door.

Winston replied excitedly, "It's so fun! I get to sit next to James. I get my

very own desk. I like Mrs. Wise. . . ."

Winston went on, but Sophie didn't hear the rest. Outside the schoolhouse, she saw Owen being greeted by another snake—probably his mom.

Sophie imagined that Owen's mom was asking Owen about *his* day at school.

And Owen did not look happy at all.

chapter 5

Snake Stories

At dinner that night, Winston told Mr. and Mrs. Mouse about the new student.

"Wow, a snake for a classmate?" Mrs. Mouse exclaimed.

Sophie nodded. "Malcolm said that snakes can be sneaky," she began.

"And Ben said they're scary!" Winston added.

"And quick-tempered," said Sophie.
"At least, that's what Piper told us."

Mrs. Mouse seemed surprised at their words as she passed the cheese biscuits. "Actually," she said calmly, "I was *going* to say: 'A snake for a

classmate? How *delightful.*'"

"Delightful?!" Sophie and Winston cried in surprise.

Mr. Mouse nodded. "Have you or any of your friends ever *met* a snake before?" he asked.

Sophie and Winston shook their heads.

Mr. Mouse smiled. "Well, *I* have," he said. "Your mother and I used to know a very nice snake."

"Yes," agreed Mrs. Mouse. "And I thought you two knew better than to make up your mind before you even get to know someone."

All of a sudden, Sophie's biscuit didn't taste so good. She thought again about Owen sitting alone at recess, and how sad he looked after school. Now she really, *really* wished she had asked Owen to play.

Later that evening, Sophie went to find her dad. George Mouse was at his design desk, working on a blueprint for a shrew family's new house.

"Dad?" Sophie said. "Would you

tell me more about the snake you and Mom knew?"

Mr. Mouse put down his pencil. He turned to look at Sophie, smiled, and ruffled the fur on her head. "Her name was Olivia," he began. "Her family lived near here when your mom and I were young. We'd play together all the time—especially over in the buttercup patch. Then, one day, when I was maybe ten, she and her family moved away. I missed her a lot. Your mom did, too."

Sophie was quiet for a moment, then she said, "Sounds like she was a very good friend of yours."

Mr. Mouse nodded. "She *was* a very good friend," he said.

Sophie shuffled to her room. She got into her pajamas, climbed into her bed, pulled up her quilt made of milkweed fluff, and turned off the light.

As she lay in the dark, Sophie made a decision.

Owen was brave enough to walk into a school full of strangers, she thought. *Tomorrow, I can be brave enough to ask him to play.*

chapter 6

Time Flies When You're Having Fun!

At school the next day, the first thing Sophie did was look for Owen. But he wasn't there.

The students took their seats. Mrs. Wise called attendance. They started their lesson.

Still no Owen.

Sophie looked back at the door many times during the day. At every rustle or creak or whoosh of the wind, she turned to see if it was Owen arriving.

But the day flew by, and Owen never appeared.

The same thing happened the next day. Everyone was in school except for Owen. Where was he?

At least it was library day, which took Sophie's mind off of it. She *loved* library day! "Each of you may check out one book this morning," Mrs. Wise told the students.

The following day, the class went on a field trip to the beautiful

Goldmoss Pond. Sophie was so excited that she didn't even notice Owen was still missing.

Before Sophie knew it, the week-end had arrived. On Saturday after-noon, she and Hattie went to help out at the bakery. Mrs. Mouse had a brand-new recipe to try out.

She was known far and wide for her unusual and tasty creations. Today's experiment was a cinnamon-spiced buttercup cake. "If it's not a ten on the Tasty Scale, it's not ready to be sold," Mrs. Mouse told the girls with a wink.

She emptied a basket onto the counter. Two delicate buttercups fell out. "Oh dear," said Mrs. Mouse. "We're definitely going to need more buttercups."

"We'll go pick some!" Sophie suggested. Hattie nodded in agreement.

The buttercup patch was very close to the bakery.

Mrs. Mouse hesitated, then said,

"Okay, but be back in half an hour."
Sophie and Hattie skipped out of
the bakery, baskets in hand.

chapter 7

one stuck mouse

Sophie and Hattie could just see over the tops of the taller flowers. They made their way out into the center of the buttercup patch. Then they looked around in all directions.

"Wow!" said Sophie. "It's like a big yellow ocean of buttercups . . . I think." Neither she nor Hattie had ever been to the ocean. There were

plenty of lakes, ponds, and streams
in Silverlake Forest, but no oceans.

They started picking the smaller

flowers. Sophie grabbed a stem, pulled, and stowed the flower in her basket. *Grab, pick, stow. Grab, pick, stow.* Sophie got into a rhythm. Her basket was soon a quarter full.

"Exactly how many buttercups do you think are in this patch?" Sophie asked Hattie over her shoulder. But Hattie didn't answer. "Hattie?"

Sophie turned. Hattie was off in a different part of the field.

Sophie went on picking. *Could it be a million buttercups?* she wondered. *A billion? Grab, pick,*

stow. Imagine the shade of yellow paint I could make from these! Maybe Mom will let me take home some extras. Buttercup yellow . . . that would be a great color to have, and not just for flower paintings. I could paint amazing sunrises! And sunsets! And cheese and—

"AAAAHHHH!" Sophie was falling! Her basket of buttercups went flying as she slid down a narrow hole in the ground. Just as suddenly, she landed with an *oof!* on the hard dirt floor.

It took a moment for Sophie to clear her head. But she wasn't hurt—just very startled. She stood up and dusted off her dress. Then she looked around. There were no side tunnels, and the top of the hole was way out of reach. She tried to get a grip so she could climb up. But the dirt just crumbled in her hands.

She needed help to get out.

"Hattie!" she called. "Haaaat-tie!"

She held her breath, listening

for Hattie's reply. None came. Now Sophie wished she and Hattie had stuck together. *She's too far away to hear me! How will I ever get out of here? Oh no. Will I be stuck down here . . . forever?*

"HATTIE!" Sophie tried again at the top of her lungs.

Sophie listened—and heard a rustle from above. "Hattie? I'm down here!"

As Sophie looked upward, a head popped into view. It was small and round and wearing a brimmed cap. And it was peering into the hole!

Then a voice called down, "Sophie Mouse? Is that you?" It was a little raspy, but also gentle.

Now Sophie was sure. It definitely wasn't Hattie.

It was Owen!

chapter 8

To the Rescue!

For a minute, Sophie was so surprised, she couldn't speak. Finally, she squeaked out, "Yes! It's me! I-I can't get out."

Owen was quiet a moment. Then he said, "I have an idea. I'll lower my tail down. Grab on. I'll pull you out!"

"Oh!" Sophie exclaimed. "Okay!"

Owen's head disappeared as he

turned around. He lowered his tail—down, down, down—until it was within Sophie's reach.

For a split second, Sophie hesitated. She was afraid to be down in the hole, alone. But she was afraid to grab on to Owen, too.

Then Sophie remembered how brave Owen had been on the first day of school.

And here he is being brave again, thought Sophie. *It's time for me to be brave, too!*

Sophie grabbed on. She felt her feet lift up off the ground. Inch by

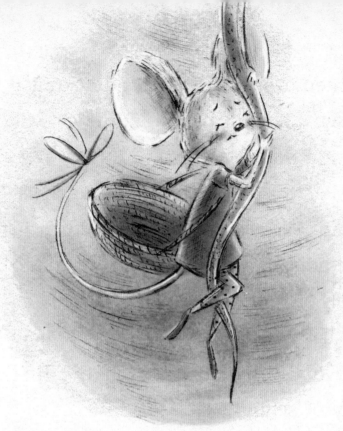

inch, Sophie rose, higher and higher. She held on tight, trying not to slip, until she could reach out and grab onto the lip of the hole. Then she scrambled up and out, safe at last!

"You saved me!" Sophie exclaimed as she got to her feet. "Thank you!"

"No problem," Owen said bashfully. "It's no big deal."

Gazing out over the buttercup patch, Sophie spotted Hattie off in the distance. Sophie waved, and Hattie came running over.

"I was so worried!" Hattie cried, huffing and puffing. "I turned around and you were gone—" She stopped, catching sight of Owen. "Oh, hi. W-what are you doing here?"

Before Owen could answer, Sophie

burst out, "Owen just saved me! I fell into this hole and he pulled me out!"

Hattie looked into the hole. "Oh my goodness," she said. She gave Sophie a hug. "I'm so glad you're okay." Then she beamed at Owen.

"Way to go, Owen!" she cried. "Quick thinking!"

Owen looked down at the ground. "I don't know . . . I just . . . well, she needed help, so I helped," he said.

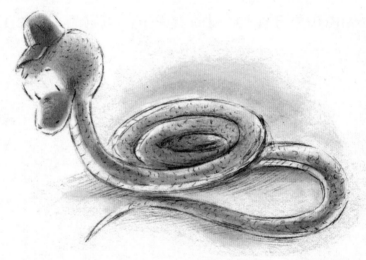

Just then, a voice from behind Sophie and Hattie made them jump. "Oh, here you are!"

Sophie and Hattie turned to see a grown-up snake towering over them. Sophie's heart skipped a beat, and Hattie reached for Sophie's hand.

But then Owen said, "Oh, hi, Mom. This is Sophie Mouse and Hattie Frog."

Looking again, Sophie recognized Owen's mother as the same grown-up who was waiting for him at school on the first day.

"Hello, Sophie. Hello, Hattie," Mrs. Snake said kindly. "Very nice to meet you. I'm Olivia."

Olivia? thought Sophie. *Olivia Snake? Wait a minute. It can't be. Or can it?*

Is she the Olivia Snake—Mom and Dad's long-lost friend?

chapter 9

Old Friends and New Friends

"Excuse me, Olivia—I mean, Mrs. Snake," said Sophie. "Did you grow up around here?"

Olivia's eyes went wide in surprise. "How did you guess?" she said with a laugh. "I used to play all the time in this very buttercup patch!"

"With George and Lily Mouse?!" Sophie asked excitedly. A speechless

Olivia Snake nodded, so Sophie added, "They're my mom and dad! My mom is at her bakery, right over there." She pointed toward town. "We were picking buttercups for a recipe she is trying out."

Suddenly, Sophie had a great idea: They could all go back to the bakery together to surprise Mrs. Mouse. Mrs. Snake loved the idea.

Hattie, Owen, and Mrs. Snake helped Sophie pick fresh buttercups to replace the ones that had scattered when she fell. Then they walked together to the bakery. Sophie and

Hattie walked in first. Mrs. Mouse was happy to see them because she had started to worry. Then Olivia and Owen came in—and Mrs. Mouse nearly dropped her cookie sheet.

"Oh, I'd know that face anywhere!" Mrs. Mouse said. "Olivia Snake!"

"Lily Mouse!" cried Olivia.

Mrs. Mouse gave Mrs. Snake a big hug while Sophie jumped and clapped for joy. Happy surprises were the best!

"Well, this calls for a celebration!" Mrs. Mouse declared.

She fixed up a tray of pastries and
made a pot of tea. Then the two
old friends sat down at a

café table to chat and catch up.

Meanwhile, Sophie, Hattie, and Owen set up their own tea party behind the counter. They took turns sneaking pastries from the grown-ups' tray.

After a few cookies, Sophie asked the question she'd been wondering all week. "Owen, how come you never came back to school?"

Owen hesitated. "Well, my mom used to be a schoolteacher," he said. "She's teaching me at home. For

now, at least." Owen looked down. "Anyway . . . I didn't think anyone liked me."

"Oh, no!" Hattie burst out. "That's not true! Not . . . exactly."

Sophie gulped, feeling embarrassed. "I think it was just, well, we were all a little nervous. None of us had ever met a snake before." She took a deep breath. "We're really sorry, Owen."

Soon it was time for the Snakes to leave.

Sophie thanked Owen again for saving her.

"Will we see you at school on Monday?" she asked.

Owen moved slowly toward the door. Then he looked back at Sophie.

"Maybe," he said with a smile.

— chapter 10 —

Better Late Than Never

Sophie tapped her pencil on her desk. She stared at the clock on the school-house wall. It was Monday morning. Mrs. Wise was about to start the first lesson.

Owen wasn't there.

Sophie looked over at Hattie, two desks away. They had saved the desk between them for Owen.

"I thought for sure he'd come," Sophie whispered to Hattie. She slumped in her chair. *I guess I was wrong.*

Just then, the door swung open. A ray of sunlight fell across the classroom. Owen hurried in. "Sorry I'm late, Mrs. Wise," he said, out of breath.

Sophie heard some of the students whisper in surprise. But this time it was *Sophie* who squeaked—from happiness.

She waved wildly to Owen. Hattie motioned for him to take the desk between them. He came over and sat down.

"We are so glad you're here!" Sophie whispered to him.

She could feel everyone looking at them—including Mrs. Wise.

Sophie's eyes met her teacher's.
Mrs. Wise winked and smiled warmly.

At recess, Sophie and Hattie led
Owen outside. "What should we
play?" Hattie asked.

Sophie shrugged. "What do you like to do, Owen? Hopscotch?"

Owen shook his head. "I'm not good at jumping," he said. "But I am good at jump *rope*."

"Huh?" said Hattie.

Owen smiled. He rested his head on the end of the bench. He propped up his tail on the base of the seesaw.

Then he twirled his body around and around. . . .

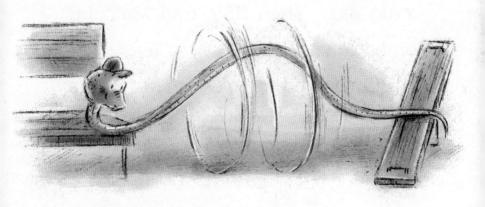

"A jump rope!" Sophie and Hattie cried, laughing.

Sophie hopped in and started singing, "School, school, the golden rule, spell your name and go to school: S-O-P-H-I-E!" She jumped out.

Hattie took her turn: "H-A-T-T-I-E!" She jumped out.

Lydie hopped over and asked if she could play. Then Ellie and Malcolm joined in.

Ben walked up to Owen as he was

twirling. "Doesn't that hurt, Owen?" Ben asked.

"Nope, not at all!" said Owen. "It's fun. I'll get tired after a while. But not yet. Jump in, if you want!"

Ben smiled and jumped in: "B-E-N!"

Before long, the whole class was playing.

116

That evening, Sophie painted a picture using her newest color, buttercup yellow. It was a landscape of the buttercup patch under a bright orange and pink sunset. In the corner, she painted a mouse, a frog, and a snake, playing together.

Sophie stepped back and studied her work. She thought it was one of her best yet!

Sophie smiled. She was happy—because of her painting, because Owen had come back to school and everyone liked him, and most of all, because she had made a new friend.

The End

Here's a peek at the next
Adventures of Sophie Mouse book!

In the heart of Silverlake Forest, a mouse, a frog, and a snake talked and played by a stream. It was just another after-school playdate for Sophie Mouse and her good friends, Hattie Frog and Owen Snake.

Owen was lazily draped over a low-hanging tree branch. He watched as Sophie, sitting on a rock below, drew in her sketchbook. She was adding a bee to her garden scene.

"That reminds me of our field trip to see the honeybee hives!" Owen said. "It was my favorite part of school this week."

Mrs. Wise, their teacher at Silverlake Elementary, had taken them to see how honey was made by the worker bees.

"Want to know *my* favorite thing from this week?" called Hattie. She was hopping from lily pad to lily pad. "It was the visit from Mr. Wallace, the flying frog!"